P9-BHX-766

The
CHRISTMAS
CAT

by Efner Tudor Holmes

illustrated by Tasha Tudor

HarperCollins*Publishers*

The Christmas Cat

Text copyright © 1976 by Efner Tudor Holmes

Illustrations copyright © 1976 by Tasha Tudor

Printed in the U.S.A. All rights reserved.

www.harperchildrens.com

Library of Congress Cataloging-in-Publication Data

Holmes, Efner Tudor. The Christmas Cat.

Summary: On one cold Christmas eve, an abandoned
cat and a little boy receive a bit of seasonal magic.

ISBN 0-690-01267-5 — ISBN 0-690-01268-3 (lib. bdg.)

ISBN 0-06-443208-4 (pbk.)

[1. Christmas—Fiction.]   I. Tudor, Tasha.   II. Title.

PZ7.H735Ch   [E]   76-14802

❖

Typography by Carla Weise

To my husband and our three sons

With my love,

—ETH

It was the day before Christmas. It had stopped snowing, but a cold wind blew through the forest, bending the trees down and piling up great gusting drifts around them. Birds sat huddled in the treetops, their little claws that clutched the branches numb with cold. Below them, deer stood clustered together, nibbling at the bark. Perhaps they thought of sunlit woods and leaf-covered bushes. But the forest lay dark and cold.

A gray cat was struggling to walk through the deep snow.
He meowed piteously. Occasionally he would stop and hold up a
paw caked with icy snow. For the cat, the wintry forest was not
only cold but also dangerous and unfriendly. Owls and foxes
were everywhere, ready to pounce on him. So far he had always
managed to hide in time.

Once he had had a home, a warm home with soft chairs to
sleep on and fresh bowls of milk for him to drink. But one day

he had come home only to find the place deserted. The door never opened for him again. Finally, after waiting in vain for several weeks, the cat left, sad and confused. He would have to seek another home.

In his travels he came upon many houses, but in each there had been a dog to chase him or another cat defending its territory.

Now, in the forest, the cat could not walk another step. He crept under a log and fell into an exhausted sleep.

At the edge of the forest was a small farm. It was a well-kept place and the little house looked festive, with a wreath on the door and candles in the windows.

Inside, Nate and Jason sat in the warm kitchen decorating gingerbread animal cookies for the Christmas tree. They felt uneasy, listening to the wind moan down the chimney and through the cracks.

"Will Santa Claus be able to come in weather like this, Nate?"
Jason asked.

"He lives at the North Pole so I'm sure he's used to this kind
of weather," his older brother replied, smiling. "And don't eat all
the icing. We have three more animals to do."

Their mother came into the kitchen. "Finish up, boys. It's
getting late, and you light the crèche tonight."

The crèche was a most special part of Christmas. It was already set up in the old brick oven beside the big fireplace. Nate's old gray plush donkey and Jason's little toy goat stood in the hay, looking at Mary and her baby. Miniature baskets of fruit stood nearby and carved wooden doves hovered in the corners.

After their father read "The Night Before Christmas" aloud, Nate and Jason each lit a candle and placed it carefully in front of the crèche. Then the whole family stood for a few moments looking at the scene, silent with their own thoughts.

A gust of wind threw snow against the windows and the candles flickered.

"I'm glad our animals are in our nice warm barn," said Nate. "Think how cold the wild animals must be. I wish I could put them in, too."

"Winter can be hard on them," his father said, "but most of them are used to it."

In the woods, the gray cat woke uneasily. The bitter wind had stopped, leaving the forest heavy with silence.

The cat crawled out from under the log and looked around cautiously. Through the treetops the sky was brilliant with stars. Somehow, the forest no longer seemed forbidding. The cat was aware of an unfamiliar feeling of peace. He heard a sound in the

far distance. An elusive music, enveloping him, beckoned deeper into the woods and he followed. As he went, other animals came, too, emerging from their dens and nests and burrows and joining him, until the forest was filled with creatures of every kind.

They moved silently together through the trees until they came to a clearing bright with moonlight. The music became louder. It was the sound of bells.

Into the clearing came two great horses pulling a low sled with wooden runners. Upon it stood a tall man with long hair and a beard. A small owl sat serenely on his shoulder and other birds flew around him. At his feet were baskets full of berries and nuts.

He smiled when he saw the animals gathered there. Drawing his horses to a stop, he stepped down from the sled and moved among the forest creatures, patting them and talking to them. Now and then he would cluck sympathetically at a lame leg or a paw that had been mangled by a trap. As he went, he scattered seeds on the ground. Squirrels clambered up onto his shoulders for handfuls of nuts. From the trees he hung pieces of suet for the birds, and he carried leafy branches for the deer.

As he came to the cat, he stopped in surprise. "Well, well, little
fellow," he said. "How did *you* come to be here? You belong in a warm
house with soft chairs to sleep on and a saucer of milk to drink."

He pulled his beard thoughtfully. "I know of a small farm
not far from here," he said. "Two little boys live there and there isn't
a finer place for an animal to live." He picked up the shivering cat

and returned to the bobsled. He stood for a moment smiling at the forest animals. Then the great horses started up and once again the music of their harness bells filled the forest.

The horses traveled swiftly, but the cat was no longer cold. He lay curled in a basket at the tall man's feet, lulled by the music of the bells.

It was Christmas morning. Their parents were still asleep when Nate and Jason raced downstairs to the big fireplace to find their stockings.

"Jason, Jason, look what's here!" called Nate softly. "It's a little cat!" And indeed, to the boys' amazement, there was a gray cat curled up in a chair close to the fire.

"But Nate, where could he have come from?" cried Jason, completely forgetting to be quiet.

"I'm not sure," said his brother, looking thoughtful. "But some unexpected—and wonderful—things can happen when it's Christmas."

The gray cat began to purr. He looked at the crèche, and for a fleeting moment, he seemed to hear again the sound of distant bells.

How to Make Nate and Jason's
Gingerbread Animal Cookies for the Christmas Tree

You will need:

1 cup butter or other shortening
1 cup brown sugar, dark or light
3 eggs, well beaten
1½ cups molasses
6 cups all-purpose flour

1½ tablespoons ground ginger
2¼ teaspoons salt
1½ teaspoons baking soda
1 teaspoon ground cinnamon

Cream shortening, add sugar, beaten eggs, molasses, and flour mixed with other dry ingredients. Chill in refrigerator for about an hour, then roll out on a flat surface and cut into animal shapes. You can cut them freehand, or make cardboard patterns to trace around, or you can use cookie cutters. Bake on cookie sheet in a preheated 350° oven for about 20 minutes. Let cool before frosting.

Note: Make a hole for ribbon *before* baking cookies if you want to hang them on the tree.

How to Make White Frosting for Cookies

You will need:

1½ cups granulated sugar
½ cup water

2 egg whites, beaten very stiff
½ teaspoon vanilla

Boil the sugar with the water until it spins a hair when dripped from a spoon. Then get someone to pour the hot syrup slowly over the two very stiffly beaten egg whites. As one pours, the other should continue to beat the egg whites, until the syrup is all used up and the frosting holds a peak. Add ½ teaspoon vanilla. Outline the animals with this frosting, and give them eyes, mouths, etc. If you don't have a pastry tube, you can make a cornucopia from a piece of strong brown or waxed paper, pinned with a pin or a toothpick. You can squeeze the frosting through this.